Brandi Chastain

Not Just One of the Boys

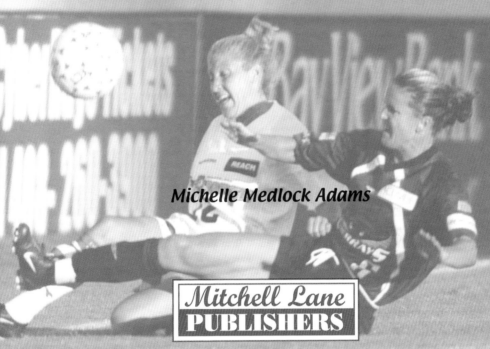

Michelle Medlock Adams

Mitchell Lane
PUBLISHERS

P.O. Box 196
Hockessin, Delaware 19707
Visit us on the web: www.mitchelllane.com
Comments? email us: mitchelllane@mitchelllane.com

Printing   1   2   3   4   5   6   7   8

A Robbie Reader
No Hands Allowed

Brandi Chastain   Brian McBride   DaMarcus Beasley
David Beckham   Freddy Adu   Josh Wolff
Landon Donovan

Library of Congress Cataloging-in-Publication Data
Adams, Michelle Medlock.
    Brandi Chastain / by Michelle Medlock Adams.
        p. cm. — (A Robbie reader. No hands allowed)
    Includes bibliographical references and index.
    ISBN 1-58415-390-3 (library bound)
    1. Chastain, Brandi. 2. Soccer players—United States—Biography—Juvenile literature.
3. Women soccer players—United States—Biography—Juvenile literature. I. Title. II. Series.
GV942.7.C52A33 2005
796.334'092—dc22
                                                                    2005004250

ABOUT THE AUTHOR: Earning first place awards from Associated Press, the Hoosier State Press Association and the Society of Professional Journalists, **Michelle Medlock Adams** has published more than 3,000 articles in newspapers and magazines around the country, such as *Writer's Digest, Today's Christian Woman, Brio,* and *American Cheerleader Magazine.* She has also authored 15 books, including her award-winning picture book, *Conversations On the Ark.* She graduated from Indiana University with a journalism degree in 1991, and she's been writing professionally ever since. She and her husband, Jeff, and their two daughters, Abby and Allyson, make their home in Texas with their three miniature dachshunds. If you wish to contact Michelle, her website address is www.michellemedlockadams.com.

PHOTO CREDITS: Cover—Richard Schultz/WireImage; pp. 1, 3, 8, 10, 14, 26—Jed Jacobsohn/Getty Images; p. 6—Mickael Kappeler/AFP/Getty Images; pp. 12, 22, 24—Tom Hauck/Getty Images; p. 18—John Ferrey/Getty Images; p. 16—Michael Stahlschmidt/Time Life Pictures/Getty Images; p. 20—Robyn Beck/Getty Images.

ACKNOWLEDGMENTS: The following story has been thoroughly researched, and to the best of our knowledge, represents a true story. While every possible effort has been made to ensure accuracy, the publisher will not assume liability for damages caused by inaccuracies in the data, and makes no warranty on the accuracy of the information contained herein. This story has not been authorized nor endorsed by Brandi Chastain nor anyone associated with Brandi Chastain.

TABLE OF CONTENTS

Brandi Chastain waves to her fans before the game against Denmark at Giants Stadium in New Jersey on November 3, 2004. She is very popular with the crowds.

Women's Soccer Goes Hollywood

Before 1999, people did not know very much about the world's best female soccer players. Few people knew much about women's soccer at all. That all changed after the 1999 Women's World Cup.

The U.S. Women's Soccer team had not won the world championship since 1991. On July 10, 1999, the U.S. beat China in a thrilling match in front of 90,000 screaming fans. President Bill Clinton personally congratulated (kun-GRAT-oo-lay-ted) the team on its victory.

It had been a great year for women's soccer. The sport had become very popular, and Brandi Chastain had become a sports hero. During that 1999 soccer season, she played in

27 games for the national team and scored five goals with five **assists**. But it was her performance in the final game against China that made her famous.

Brandi scored a goal on a penalty kick after the second overtime of the game. She

Brandi Chastain eyes the soccer ball during the Olympic Games in 2004. She is pictured here with Brazilian forward Cristiane.

celebrated big time! A photographer snapped a picture of that celebration. She was pictured on her knees, mouth wide open, eyes closed, fists in the air, wearing a black sports bra and white soccer shorts. She appeared on the cover of *Time, Newsweek, People,* and *Sports Illustrated.* Some have called that penalty kick one of the greatest moments in the history of women's sports. Even people who weren't soccer fans knew about Brandi—the soccer star in the sports bra.

Brandi became an instant **icon** (EYE-kon). Suddenly, young people everywhere began writing her letters and e-mails. Some boys even asked Brandi to marry them! Brandi said in an interview, "It was definitely overwhelming, and there was no way I could have prepared for it. . . . It's so amazing how the **media** can change everybody's **perception** of you so quickly."

It was a new day for women's soccer and a new day for Brandi. She had become a soccer superstar. Her teammates had always called her Hollywood, as a funny nickname. Now, her nickname seemed to really fit.

7

Brandi is a very physical player. Here she is, giving it her all, during a Women's United Soccer Association (WUSA) game at Spartan Stadium on April 5, 2003.

Just One of the Boys

Brandi Denise Chastain was born on July 21, 1968, in San Jose, California. Her parents were Lark and Roger Chastain. Lark and Roger had been high school sweethearts. They married and started a family. After Brandi, they had a son, named Chad.

Growing up, Brandi played sports with her brother. She definitely wasn't a "girly girl." She played on all-boys baseball and football teams.

When Brandi started playing soccer, none of her family or friends played.

"I had no role models to inspire me on the field," she writes in her book, *It's Not About the Bra: How to Play Hard, Play Fair, and Put the Fun Back into Competitive Sports.* Then, she saw the San Jose Earthquakes, a men's

Here Brandi chases down the ball during the final WUSA game against the Boston Breakers. Due to a lack of money, the WUSA came to an end in 2003. Brandi would like to see the professional women's soccer league begin again.

professional (pro-FEH-shuh-nul) soccer team, play. She found her role models on that great team.

She dreamed of becoming a pro soccer player. She knew it would take lots of practice. Still, she wanted to become the best soccer player she could be.

When she was 11, Brandi attended soccer camp. Tim Schultz, who played for the Earthquakes, was one of the camp **counselors**. Brandi wanted to prove she was as good as any of the boys. When her team lost one afternoon, Brandi pouted (POW-ted). Schultz called out, "Deal with it!"

Those words stuck with Brandi. Even today when she gets upset on the field, she tells herself, "Deal with it." At age 11, she had learned that pouting wasn't going to make her a better player.

11

Brandi is a very passionate player. She loves to play well, and she loves to celebrate playing well. Here she celebrates scoring a goal against the New York Power.

More Life Lessons

Brandi was a soccer star in high school. She led her team, Archbishop Mitty High School, to three straight state championships. She went on to play college soccer at the University of California at Berkeley. She did very well. She was named the Soccer America Freshman Player of the Year. This is a very important award.

Then she hurt herself playing soccer and had to have an operation on her knee. She couldn't play in 1987 or 1988. This was difficult for Brandi because she missed playing very much. In 1989, she transferred to Santa Clara University.

Everyone expected a lot from Brandi. People thought of her as a great player. She felt

One of the strongest female soccer players in the world, Brandi commands the field. Here she volleys a pass during a game against the Boston Breakers.

she had something to prove. Brandi had to work hard to get back into shape after her injury. Sometimes her attitude wasn't good. Her coach at Santa Clara didn't like bad attitudes.

He told Brandi he didn't want her on the team if she couldn't be a good sport. She was mad and hurt. This was another **turning point** for Brandi. She thought about his words and decided to change her attitude. Her coach agreed to take her back onto the team.

From that day on, Brandi was different. She stopped complaining and started working very hard. She became a team player. She led the Santa Clara Broncos to two **final four** appearances. She was ready to be great on and off the soccer field.

15

They say nothing tastes as sweet as victory. Brandi (left) and teammate Tisha Venturini (right) kiss the Founders Cup Championship Trophy just to be sure.

CHAPTER FOUR

Living Her Dreams

Brandi played very well in college. She scored 32 goals and had eight **assists** in three college soccer seasons. In 1990, she graduated from Santa Clara University with a degree in television and communications.

In 1991, her dreams continued coming true. She made the World Championship U.S. Women's National Team. In 1993, she played on the West Team at the U.S. Olympic Festival in San Antonio, Texas. Her team won the gold medal—the very highest honor!

Brandi won many awards. She gained many fans. Her biggest fans were her parents. Her mom and dad cheered for her from the sidelines. Brandi's mom had been a cheerleader when she was young. At Brandi's

17

Brandi Chastain (left) and Mia Hamm (right)—two of the most famous female soccer players to ever take the field— sport their medals after winning third place honors at the FIFA 2003 Women's World Cup match.

Brandi's Many Hats

In 1997, Brandi married her college soccer coach, Jerry Smith. She became a stepmother to Jerry's son, Cameron, who also plays soccer. Jerry is still the head coach for women's soccer at Santa Clara University. Brandi is assistant coach.

Getting married didn't keep Brandi off the soccer field. In 1997, she played women's club soccer for the Sacramento Storm. Her team became the Western Regional Champions that year. In the summer of 1998, Brandi helped the U.S. National Team win its first-ever gold medal at the Goodwill Games. And 1999 brought the famous win in the Women's World Cup. Brandi continues to play for the U.S. National Team.

Brandi has loved soccer from the very first moment she played the game. In fact, she remembers sleeping in her first soccer uniform for two weeks straight.

Brandi and her 1999 World Cup teammates helped found the Women's United Soccer Association (WUSA). This was the only professional women's soccer league in the United States. Their first official season began in 2001. Brandi played for the Bay Area CyberRays until the WUSA stopped holding games. The WUSA was not making enough money and had to close at the end of 2003. Many people, including Brandi, want to see the WUSA start again. With enough support, that could happen.

Even though Brandi can't play soccer professionally right now, she has other ways to earn a living. Chastain signed a million-dollar contract with Nike. Other companies also asked her to pose with their products.

Later, Brandi was able to combine her love of sports with her college degree. The FOX network asked her to serve as a **correspondent** (kor-reh-SPON-dent) for the show *NFL Under the Helmet.* She reports on various National Football League (NFL) players.

Brandi Chastain (right), whose favorite number is 6, isn't afraid to play rough if that's what is needed. Here she pushes Emmy Barr (center) while goalkeeper Siri Mullinix (left) makes a save.

Brandi has other interests as well. She enjoys visiting pet shelters, playing Scrabble on her computer, hanging out with her family and friends, running with her dogs, and learning new languages. She also likes playing golf and snowboarding.

In June 2004, Brandi read a magazine article about youth sports. She was shocked to read that parents who watched their kids on the field would yell mean things to the players and their coaches. Even more frightening, some people would start fistfights on the field. She asked Gloria Averbuch to help her find a solution to this troubling problem. The result was their book, *It's Not About the Bra: How to Play Hard, Play Fair, and Put the Fun Back into Competitive Sports.*

Today, Brandi is an active soccer mom, wife, coach, player, author, and more. She also spends time teaching children about soccer and raising money for **charities**. She has played on the television game shows *Jeopardy!* and *The Weakest Link.* The money she won

benefited her favorite charity, the Children's Cancer Research Fund.

Those who are closest to Brandi say she is a very special person. Her talent and love for the sport has made women's soccer very popular around the world.

Brandi (right) and opponent Kerry Collins (left) of the Philadelphia Charge both dive for the ball. They're not afraid to get dirty.

1968 Brandi Denise Chastain born July 21 in San Jose, California

1986 Enrolls at the University of California, Berkeley; is named the Soccer America Freshman Player of the Year

1989 Transfers to Santa Clara University and leads the soccer team to two final four NCAA appearances

1990 Graduates from Santa Clara University

1991 Represents the United States on the soccer field for the first time on April 18 against Mexico

1993 Participates on the U.S. team in championships in New York; joins the West Team, which wins the gold medal at the Texas Olympic Festival; is cut from the national team

1995 Makes the women's national soccer team again

1996 Participates in the Olympic Games in Atlanta, where the Americans win the gold medal

1997 Marries long-time sweetheart Jerry Smith and becomes stepmother to his son, Cameron

1999 Becomes a household name after the famous penalty kick that helps her team beat China in the Women's World Cup; signs a million-dollar contract with Nike

2001 Begins playing for the Bay Area CyberRays in the first official season of the WUSA, a league she and her World Cup teammates helped found

2003 WUSA suspends the women's soccer league; Brandi continues to play for the U.S. National Team

2004 Her book, *It's Not About The Bra: How to Play Hard, Play Fair, and Put the Fun Back into Competitive Sports,* is published

2005 Appeared on "Celebrity Poker Showdown" on February 22 on Bravo

GLOSSARY

assists (ah-SISTS)—when a player passes off to another player who scores for the team.

charities (CHAIR-eh-tees)—organizations that provide money to help the needy or sick.

correspondent (kor-reh-SPON-dent)—a journalist who reports news from a particular place or on a particular subject.

counselors (KOWN-seh-lers)—people, usually adults, who help run summer or sports camps.

final four (FINE-l FOR)—the four best teams left after other tournaments; they play against one another to determine the champion.

icon (EYE-kon)—an object of attention and devotion.

media (ME-dee-uh)—the group of communication outlets such as newspapers, television, magazines, and radio.

megaphone (MEG-ah-fone)—a cone-shaped device that is held up to the mouth to make a person's voice louder.

perception (per-SEP-shun)—the way a person feels about or looks at something.

pouted (POW-ted) to sulk and complain when things do not go your way.

professional (pro-FEH-shuh-nul)—a person who is paid to perform.

teenage (TEEN-age)—a word to describe a person who is 13 to 19 years old.

turning point (TERN-ing poynt)—an important time or event in a person's life that causes the person to act or think differently.

Articles

Chastain, Brandi. "The Biggest Game of My Life." http://sportsillustrated.cnn.com/sifor women/issue_three/dear_diary/brandi

Golf Life: "Brandi Chastain: U.S. Women's Soccer Star, Bunker Threat," March 2004. www.travelandleisure.com/tlgolf/invoke. cfm?ObjectID=9E1294D6-D858-456B-B8E9458D8AE3FC45

Web Addresses

Brandi's homepage
www.itsnotaboutthebra.com

Women's Soccer World Online, "Chastain, Brandi"
www.womensoccer.com/biogs/ chastain.html

Women's United Soccer Association
www.wusa.com

U.S. Soccer
www.ussoccer.com

Works Consulted

Buckheit, Mary. "Brandi Chastain." ESPN.com, Page 2, © 2002
http://espn.go.com/page2/s/questions/chastain010618.html

Chastain, Brandi, with Gloria Averbuch. *It's Not About The Bra: How to Play Hard, Play Fair, and Put the Fun Back into Competitive Sports.* New York: HarperCollins, 2004.

Soccer Times, "Brandi Chastain,"
www.soccertimes.com/usteams/roster/women/chastain.htm

WUSA: "Brandi Chastain"
www.wusa.com/festival/team/?id=1071&top_team_id=248